BEDTIME STORIES
for the
Very Young

SELECTED BY SALLY GRINDLEY
· ILLUSTRATED BY CHRIS FISHER ·

Kingfisher

For Gina S.G.
For Jannie C.F.

KINGFISHER
An imprint of Larousse plc
Elsley House, 24-30 Great Titchfield Street
London W1P 7AD

This edition published by Kingfisher 1995
2 4 6 8 10 9 7 5 3
This selection copyright © Sally Grindley 1993
Illustrations copyright © Chris Fisher 1991, 1993

Fussy © Anne Fine 1991
A Lullaby for Freddy © Adèle Geras 1991
A Dragon's Bedtime © Judy Hindley 1991
Ella's Bedtime Story © Leon Rosselson 1991
The King of the Blue Lagoon © Ann Turnbull 1991
The Lamb Who Couldn't Sleep © John Yeoman 1991

Material in this edition was previously published
by Kingfisher Books in 1991 and 1993 in
Bedtime Stories for the Very Young.

A CIP catalogue record for this book
is available from the British Library

ISBN 1 85697 339 5

Designed by Tony Potter
Printed in Hong Kong / China

Contents

A LULLABY FOR FREDDY

Adèle Geras

When Freddy the Fearless moved into the doll's house there was great excitement.

"He's a soldier," said Keith the little velvet frog. "I expect he'll have all kinds of stories to tell."

"He's bound to be tremendously brave," said Baby, the painted wooden doll who never moved from the wooden cradle.

"And strong," said Minna the rag doll. "Have you seen how tall and straight he stands in his shiny blue and gold uniform? And isn't that a sword strapped round his waist?"

Freddy the Fearless turned out to be every bit as brave and strong as Baby and Minna had hoped. He was also very talkative, just as Keith had said he would be.

"I expect," Freddy said, on the very first day, "that all of you are longing to hear tales of my soldiering, my bravery, assorted sagas of fights and battles and so on,

aren't you? I mean, this is an extremely pleasant doll's house, and they do say a change is as good as a rest, but it's not quite what I'm used to, oh no indeed!"

"Did you live in a barracks?" Minna wanted to know.

"In a fort," answered Freddy the Fearless, his voice full of pride. "A splendid cardboard fort in the middle of a sandy desert. There were palm trees and camels and we had battles in the morning. In the afternoon we marched around and had parades, and in the evening we all lined up on the floor of the fort for a spot of shut-eye. Oh, those were the days!"

"Where are all the other soldiers now?" Baby asked.

"Gone," said Freddy sadly. "Every last one. Dropped behind chests of drawers, exchanged for cars and things, taken away and given to jumble sales if there was anything wrong with them at all, even the slightest scratch . . . oh, there have been so many casualties!"

"Well, we lead a very quiet life here," said Keith. "In the daytime, sometimes we are played with and sometimes we aren't."

"What do you do when you're not being played with?" Fearless Freddy wanted to know.

"We chat," said Baby. "There's always plenty to chat about."

"Oh, I'm just the chap you need then," said Freddy. "I know wonderful stories. I'll keep you amused for hours."

And he did. The first day simply flew past, and Minna, Keith and Baby heard about the Adventure of the Dining-room Table, and the Battle of the Desk, when Freddy rode on the back of a wooden elephant through tropical jungles of pencil trees. Then there was the time when he fell into the basin and bobbed about in the water for a full ten minutes before being rescued.

Then the night time came, but it wasn't really dark in the doll's house. There were comforting patches of golden light from the landing which shone into the room and into the windows of the doll's house as well. Keith rested his head on one of his pink velvet legs and prepared to dream of waterlilies. Baby stared at the pattern in the ceiling and wondered what she could pretend it was tonight. Minna flopped into the corner and listened to the night noises.

"That's a strange sound," she said to herself. "It's just like someone crying. But Baby doesn't cry, and neither does Keith, and everyone knows that brave soldiers never, never cry. Who can it be?"

The snuffling went on and on, quite softly at first, and then louder and louder ... boo ... hoo ... boo ... hoo.

"Is that you, Baby?" Minna whispered.

"No," Baby said.

"Is it you, Keith?"

"No," said Keith. "You woke me up. I was dreaming of waterlilies."

"Is it you Fearless Freddy?"

"I'm afraid it is," came Freddy's voice out of the corner where he'd been put. "I'm sorry to say it is."

"But what's the matter?" asked Baby.

"I'm frightened."

"How can you be frightened?" Keith said. "There are no enemies here, and no battles. There isn't anything to be frightened of."

"Yes there is," said Freddy. "I'm frightened of the dark."

Minna, Baby and Keith thought about this for a moment.

"It isn't even properly dark," said Minna at last. "Look, there's a triangle of golden light shining through the door. Can you see?"

"But there are still dark corners," said Fearless Freddy. "And shadows. What's that, for instance? That big, square shadow just over there?"

"I expect it's my cradle," said Baby, "making a black patch on the wall."

"Isn't there anything we can do?" asked Keith. "What did you do in the fort?"

"Our general sang us a lullaby," said Freddy. "Only don't tell anyone I told you."

8

"And did that help you not to be scared of the dark?" Minna asked.

"Oh yes," said Freddy. "It had special words, but I can't remember what they are. If only I could remember, I'd be all right, I know I would."

"I know lots of lullabies," said Minna. "Every night I'll sing some of the lullabies I know and perhaps that will help."

"Good show!" said Freddy, not sounding in the least bit scared. "Sing away!"

So Minna sang Freddy all her very best and sleepiest-sounding special lullabies. Then she whispered, "Are you still frightened, Freddy?"

The only answer was the buzz of snores coming from Fearless Freddy's corner. He was fast asleep.

"He must be all right, after all," said Minna. "Goodnight everyone."

No one answered. Minna heard only the snuffles of a dreaming frog and the soft breathing of a baby in her cradle. She closed her eyes and went to sleep till morning.

Hush-a-bye baby on the tree top.
When the wind blows the cradle will rock;
When the bough breaks, the cradle will fall;
Down will come baby, cradle and all.

FUSSY

Anne Fine

Fussy was tired. His eyes were drooping and his thumb kept creeping into his mouth. But before he could go to bed he had to find his special yellow blanket.

And then he needed Elephant with his big flappy ears, in case he was lonely.

And then he needed the huge, shiny picture book you could wipe clean, in case he wanted to look at the pictures.

And he wanted his mobile aeroplanes spinning round and round above his head – No! He wanted them stopped.

And then Fussy wanted some water in the cup with the top with the little holes, in case he was thirsty.

And he wanted the fat round pebble he found on the beach one day.

And he wanted the curtains closed so he couldn't see the creepy, wavy branches on the tree outside the window –

No! He wanted them open so he *could* see the creepy,

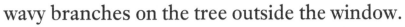

wavy branches on the tree outside the window.

And he wanted his family of pink rabbits, and all his furry glove puppets, and his bright wooden bricks.

And he wanted his light off –

No! He wanted his light back on again.

And he wanted his telephone with the long, red loopy wire, and his sailing boat, and his zoo animals, and the shiny winter jacket Gran bought him on Saturday, and his green plastic frog, and his truck and his toy cars, and his pretend bottle of beer.

And then, at last, everything was *just right*. It was exactly how he wanted it. So Fussy shut his eyes and fell asleep.

PHEW!

He slept for two whole hours. First he rolled all the way over. Then he rolled all the way back. Then he kicked about a bit.

So the rabbit family got all mixed up with the furry glove puppets. And the bright wooden bricks fell into the back of the truck. And the long, red loopy wire of the telephone tangled in the boat's sails. And the toy cars slid down the sleeves of the shiny winter jacket Gran bought him on Saturday. And the fat round pebble he found on the beach one day knocked over the huge,

shiny picture book you could wipe clean, so it fell on the green plastic frog. And water dripped out of the holes in the top of the cup onto the heads of all the animals from his zoo.

And Elephant nearly disappeared completely under the yellow blanket with the pretend bottle of beer . . .

What a mess! What a *terrible* mess! It certainly wasn't just right any more. It wasn't how Fussy wanted it at all.

But when he woke up, did he mind? No. Not a bit!

You see he wasn't fussy any more. He'd had his nap!

A DRAGON'S BEDTIME

Judy Hindley

Long, long ago – before your grandmother was born, before cities were built, before there were even any people in the world – a family of dragons began their dragon day.

"Eat up," said Daryll's mum. "You need your breakfast. It's going to be a long day for you."

You've probably heard people talk about having a long day. You may have wondered what on earth they mean. Well, when Daryll's mum said 'long', she meant LONG. A dragon's day is not an ordinary day. The day of a dragon lasts for seven thousand YEARS.

Imagine playing for seven thousand years, without a nap!

Of course, to a dragon, it seems different. To a dragon, normal days come and go, blip, blip, blip! Like a light going on and off, on and off. Between the blips of daytime, stars wheel and flicker and go out again, like bursts of fireworks. Whole years go by very quickly, blowing hot and cold as the summers turn to winters. It would seem very peculiar to you and me but, to a dragon, this is just the way things are.

Today, however, Daryll was rather nervous. It was going to be a special day for him – his first day on his own without his parents.

To look at him you might not have guessed, but in fact, Daryll was just a baby. Though he was tall as a church and long as a football field, he was only young and small, as dragons go. "What shall I DO?" he whimpered, clinging to his mother. (You can just imagine how big SHE was.)

"Oh, you'll have fun," she said. "Come on, Daryll. You KNOW how often you've asked to stay alone. Why not build a mountain range? Or find a lake?"

The lake was a cheering thought. Like any baby, Daryll was particularly fond of water. What a wonderful mess he could make, all on his own!

"WE WON'T BE FAR," thundered his dad. "CALL IF YOU NEED US."

So Daryll hugged them both, and said goodbye.

The minute they were out of sight, he found a lake and jumped straight into it.

What a splash! Just think about it. Imagine a whole school going up into the air and coming down, CRASH, SPLASH! into a lake. High in the clouds, flying eagles got their stomachs wet, and wondered if it was raining, upside-down.

Soon, the water in the lake was all outside it. For miles around, there was nothing but squishy mud. Then, Daryll wallowed in the mud. There was no one to tell him not to. It was wonderful.

Time passed. In fact, a thousand years passed very quickly, while Daryll played. Before he was bored with mud, the squishy, flattish place had become a swamp, crawling with snakes and alligators. Coloured birds flew squawking from tree to tree.

Then he moved on. Just a bit further away, the sea began. To a sticky, mud-covered dragon, it looked delicious. He waded in, causing floods along the seashore. He washed all over, and floated for a while, just thinking.

Then, he had a really great idea. He dived deep down. With his great claws, he began to dig the seabed, piling enormous fistfuls of sand and mud into a wall. He was making a deep, wide hole, under the sea. He dived and dug, dived and dug, dived and dug.

When he finally stood up and looked around, the whole of the seashore looked completely different. The wall of sea mud joined the shore like a long, curved arm. Daryll had made a bay!

Outside the arm of the bay, the waves from the open sea still crashed and battered. But inside, the sea was still and sleepy. Already, groups of seals were bathing there.

Meanwhile, the bottom of the bay was now so deep that the little waves could hardly crawl up to the shore. Miles and miles of clean, new sand were showing. It was lovely. Daryll had made a beach.

Now, he was ready to try the mountain range. He had a plan.

As you know (though you may possibly have forgotten), dragons can fly. Daryll hadn't done it for a while, so he had to practise first. He flapped his wings, and ran until he got a good speed, and took off, wheeling around the sky until his wings felt nice and easy.

Then, as he flew, he put down his head and stretched his arms out like a swimmer, pointing his front claws straight ahead, like the teeth of a digger. Then he dived.

BBBRRRR!!!!!! Daryll's claws ploughed up the earth into a huge, great ditch. On either side, the earth piled up at speed. The air was filled with dirt and dust and flying boulders.

Daryll ploughed that ditch again and again. At either side, a row of hills began to grow – getting bigger and bigger, till they were twice as high as Daryll.

The ditch became a deep and narrow valley. The rows of hills began to grow into two mountain ranges.

Then, suddenly, there was a roar. Daryll looked back. A wall of water was rushing straight towards him!

Without knowing it, he had ploughed through the side of an underground lake. Now, the lake had burst into the narrow valley. Here it came, rushing down to the distant sea! Daryll scrambled out, just in time.

He had made a river!

He sat on one of the smaller of his hills, breathing hard until he had got his breath back. Then, he stretched out his ankles into the water. The water rushed over them, cold and tingly. It was gorgeous. His own shining, brand-new river!

Daryll was terribly excited now. And he was tired, too.

He wanted to SHOW somebody. He wanted his mum and dad.

"Now remember," his dad had said to him that morning. "Whenever you want us, you only have to call."

He didn't want to call. Why didn't they come for him? Why didn't they just KNOW that it was time!

He sulked. He sniffed. He felt forgotten. A great, big dragon tear rolled down his face, and hit the hill below.

But what had happened to that hill? Already, a forest had crept over it. Trees had grown up, halfway to his knees. It was beautiful.

"Dad!" called Daryll. "Mum! Come and see what I did! COME AND SEE!"

From far away, came a low, tremendous roar, like a growl of thunder. It was Daryll's dad, calling back to him, "WE'RE COMING, DARYLL!"

Thump, thump. The earth was trembling with their running footsteps. Birds went squawking, and the sky was darkening.

And look! There was his great, green, wonderful, frightful mother – a vast and shining lady dragon, as big as a mountain. Behind her was his enormous dragon father – I can't begin to say how big HE was.

Daryll leaped up onto his mother's back. Together the three of them looked at what he had made – his swamp, his beautiful bay, his shining river.

"WELL DONE, MY LAD!" thundered Daryll's father. The three of them hugged each other, and Daryll's father thumped his scaly back.

"And NOW," said Daryll's mother, "bath – and bed!"

They bathed in the sea until they felt all clean and fresh.

"What a lovely bay you made," said Daryll's mother. "Let's camp here tonight."

"WHY NOT?" thundered Daryll's dad.

For supper, they ate a forest or two, since they were vegetarian. Then they settled down. They stretched out

their tails into the cool, refreshing sea, and laid their heads on some convenient little hills. Their great bodies sank into the soft, deep sand of Daryll's beach as though it was an enormous feather bed.

"Now, isn't this nice?" said Daryll's mum.

"Mmm," said Daryll. He was almost asleep already.

Daryll's dad yawned an enormous yawn. He said, "What a day it's been! I could sleep for SEVEN THOUSAND YEARS!"

And they did.

The next time you go to the seashore, take a look. You might just see the three of them sleeping there.

THE LAMB WHO COULDN'T SLEEP

John Yeoman

It was Springtime on the marshes, and every day the young lambs raced around the fields and jumped and turned in the air. Every evening, they settled down beside their mothers, out of the wind, and fell fast asleep.

All except one.

He could never get to sleep at the right time. Instead, he would lie awake listening to the snores coming from all the other sheep in the field. No matter how hard he tried, he just didn't seem to be able to fall asleep. What was worse, just as the first faint light of the sun began to appear over the hedge and the mist began to clear from the field, he would start to doze off.

Every morning began the same way.

"Time to get up," said his mother. "It's going to be a lovely morning. Have a little drink and nibble some fresh grass and then you can go off and play with your friends."

Through his sleepy, half-opened eyes, the lamb could see some of his friends already at their leaping and spinning around the field.

"I don't think I want to play yet," he said, and gave a big yawn.

"Oh dear," said his mother. "Didn't you sleep very well?"

"No," he said. "I didn't sleep at all. I never do."

"Why don't you try counting sheep tonight?" his mother suggested.

That night he took his mother's advice. As he snuggled down beside her, sheltered from the breeze, he began to count. Because he was a very young lamb he could only count up to three, but he thought that counting up to three over and over again was probably as good as counting up to a hundred once.

"One, two, THREE ... one, two, THREE ... one, two, THREE ... one, two, THREE."

"What does that young idiot think he's doing?" came the voice of a sheep out of the darkness.

"Sounds like he's starting a race," came a reply.

"Is he trying to get us to join in a song?" suggested another.

"I think you're keeping the others awake," his mother whispered. "That's enough counting for tonight."

The lamb just sighed, rested his chin on his front feet, and settled down to another sleepless night.

After breakfast the next morning he staggered across the field to say hello to his friends. But his eyes were so

bleary and his legs were so unsteady that he stumbled right into a big oak tree.

"It isn't good manners to go bumping into people's homes like that," said a voice from above.

The lamb looked up and saw an owl sitting on a branch.

"I'm very sorry," said the lamb. "I'm so tired that I didn't see the tree."

"How can you be tired?" snapped the owl. "You haven't done anything yet!"

"I didn't sleep. I never do."

"Deary me," said the owl, in a softer voice. "We shall have to do something about that. Come back to see me this afternoon, and I'll give you some of my special sleeping mixture."

"Oh, thank you," said the lamb.

And he set off to join his friends, feeling much better already.

Back at the oak tree after lunch, he was a little disappointed to find that the owl hadn't been able to make his special sleeping mixture.

"It's nearly ready," the bird explained, "but I'm afraid I'm short of one or two items. Would you be good enough to bring me a feather which has dropped from a crow, please? That fellow over there has a loose one sticking out, do you see?"

The lamb raced after the crow, which waited until he was near before flying up and landing a few feet away. The lamb gave chase again and the crow did exactly the same thing. It happened again and again, until finally the feather came free and fluttered to the ground.

Quick as a flash the lamb picked it up in his mouth and ran back to the tree.

"Well done," said the owl. "Just leave it there while you go for the other thing."

"You mean there's more?" panted the lamb.

"Well, you want the mixture to work properly, don't you?" asked the owl. Yes, the lamb certainly wanted the mixture to work properly.

"Good," said the owl. "Now, you see that black lamb over there? He's got a particular kind of thistle sticking

to his fleece. Just bring me that, and then we're ready."

The lamb bounded off again. When the black lamb saw him coming, he thought it was a game and raced away as fast as he could. They ran and ran, this way and that across the field, for ages and ages – until finally the thistle dropped off and the lamb was able to pick it up.

He returned to the tree, all hot and puffed out.

"That's exactly what we need," said the owl. "Unfortunately, it's too late this afternoon to finish making the mixture. But you shall have it tomorrow. Go back to your mother now."

It was getting dark when the lamb got back to his mother.

"Had a nice afternoon?" she asked.

And do you know, he was so worn out that he just lay down and fell asleep.

The next morning he was completely refreshed from his good night's sleep and couldn't wait to tell the owl.

"I slept soundly all night!" he said.

"I thought you might," said the owl, with a wink. "So you won't be needing my mixture after all. You see, it's my belief that you'll sleep well every night from now on."

And the wise old owl was right. The lamb spent every day chasing around with his friends, and every night he fell sound asleep as soon as he closed his eyes.

And I hope you do, too.

ELLA'S BEDTIME STORY

Leon Rosselson

"Ella," called Michael.

"I'm asleep," said Ella and gave a loud snore.

"I can't sleep," said Michael. "The wind's blowing noises in my ears."

"You wanted to go camping," said Ella.

"The ground's hard," complained Michael. "And there are slugs everywhere."

"No there aren't," said Ella. "You're just imagining."

"Tell me a story," Michael said in a song-song voice.

Ella groaned. "You tell me a story for a change."

"But you're supposed to look after me when Mum and Dad aren't here."

"Who says?"

"Mum says. Look after Michael, she says, 'cos he's only little." Michael giggled.

Ella stared at the roof of their little tent. "I'm never going to be a mum," she said.

"You'll have to be," said Michael. "You're a girl."

"I will not," said Ella.

"Well, what will you be when you grow up?"

Ella thought. "A juggler," she said, finally.

"You can't juggle."

"Who says?"

"I've never seen you juggle. When have you ever juggled?"

"You'd be surprised," Ella said mysteriously.

"I'm going to be an elephant-tamer," said Michael.

"Humph," said Ella. "I've never seen you tame elephants."

"You'd be surprised," sang Michael and laughed.

"In a circus?"

"Everywhere. Wherever there's an elephant to tame, they'll send for me because only I know the magic word."

"What magic word?"

"Sausages! And when the elephant hears that word, he'll stop stamping his feet and throwing people about and he'll kneel in front of me and – "

"What?"

"Be tamed."

"A likely story," said Ella.

"Suffering sausages," Michael said. "Your turn."

"Once upon a time – "

"Not a fairy story," groaned Michael.

"Once upon a time," Ella insisted, "there was a little girl called Ella."

"Your name's Ella," said Michael.

"So it is," she said. "Well, this girl, Ella, lived in a castle with her Mum and Dad and little brother and she was, everybody thought, the most beautiful girl in the world."

"Humph," said Michael.

"It's my story," said Ella.

"I only said 'humph'," said Michael, putting his thumb in his mouth.

"The most beautiful girl in the world," Ella repeated. "Everyone wanted to marry her. But she wasn't interested in marrying because what she most wanted was to juggle.

"'You can't juggle,' said her Dad. 'You only have to get out of bed to trip over the carpet. How can you juggle?'

"'You can't juggle,' said her Mum. 'You only have to sit at the breakfast table to upset a bowl of cornflakes. How can you juggle?'

"'You can't juggle,' said her little brother. 'I only have to throw a ball for you to drop it. How can you juggle?'

"But Ella was stubborn. 'I will juggle,' she said to herself. And she took three ripe plums from the plum

tree and threw them into the air. Split, splat, splot. Three squashed plums lying on the earth. So she picked three red apples from the apple tree and tried juggling with those. Biff, baff, boff. Three bruised apples lying on the grass. But she wouldn't give up. She tried with stones. She tried with sticks. She tried with tennis balls. She tried with footballs. She tried with hats, shoes, bricks, weetabix, chocolate drops, cherry stones, lollipops and bars of soap. Once she tried with her Mum's best teacups. Crish, crash, crosh. Bits of china all over the kitchen floor. Was her Mum cross! But it was no good. She couldn't juggle. Poor Ella. She was very sad. And even being the most beautiful girl in the world didn't make up for it.

"One day, the doorbell rang."

"Ding-dong," said Michael from his sleeping bag.

"'Who's that?' said her Mum.

"'I expect it's just someone wanting to marry me,' said Ella. 'It usually is.' She was practising juggling with three balls of wool. That's all she was allowed to juggle with now so she couldn't do any more damage.

"'Go and answer it, then,' said her Mum. 'You and your juggling. It's about time you did something useful. Why when I was your age –'

"But Ella was off down the long stairway that led to the castle door.

"The bell rang again."

"Ding-dong," said Michael.

"Ella opened the door. There in front of her was the strangest-looking little man she'd ever seen. He had blue hair, a perfectly round face that shone like the sun, eyes as bright as silver and rainbow-coloured clothes.

"'Are you the most beautiful girl in the world?' he asked.

"'That's me,' said Ella.

"'I've come from far away to see you,' said the man.

"'Where's far away?' asked Ella.

"'High, high in the sky and over the moon,' replied the man. 'And now at last I've seen you, I can return to my own home and tell everybody I've seen –'

"'Yes, yes,' said Ella. 'But can you teach me to juggle?'

"'Of course,' he said. And reaching into the air, he plucked out a ball.

"'What colour is this?' he asked.

"'Orange,' said Ella.

"'Like the sun,' said the strange man. And reaching into the air, he plucked out another ball.

"'Blue,' said Ella.

"'Like the moon,' said the man.

"Ella frowned. 'The moon isn't blue,' she said.

"'It is where I come from,' he said. Then he reached up and drew out a third ball.

"'Silver,' said Ella.

" 'Like the morning star. Throw those into the air and they will soar and swoop and circle and spin but they will never fall to earth.' And he handed the balls to Ella.

" 'Thank you,' she said. 'Will you stay for tea?'

"But he was gone.

"Ella looked doubtfully at the three balls. Orange, blue and silver. She took the orange ball and threw it high into the air. Then the blue ball. Then the silver ball. They soared and swooped and circled and span down into her hands and up again, soaring and swooping and circling and spinning; but never, never did they fall to earth.

"Her father saw her as he came home from work. 'Wonder of wonders,' he said. 'Our Ella's juggling.'

"Her mother came running from the castle kitchen. 'Wonder of wonders,' she said. 'Our Ella can juggle.'

"Her brother came racing from the castle garden. 'Wonder of wonders,' he said. 'Our Ella's a juggler.'

"And, with the balls still soaring and swooping and circling and spinning over her head, Ella skipped out of the castle and down the hill and into the village square, where she made the orange and silver and blue balls dance brilliant patterns in the sky while the crowds of people watched and wondered and told each other that they had never, in all their born days, seen juggling like it."

There was a long silence.

"Michael," called Ella quietly.

But there was no reply from his sleeping bag; Michael was asleep.

Ella, snuggling deep into her own sleeping bag, listened to the quietness of the night. Beyond the curving roof of the tent, she thought she could see the round moon shining. If she stood up and reached out, she would be able to touch the moon. She saw herself growing tall and reaching out and touching the moon and then unhooking it from the sky and sending it soaring and spinning into space. Then she reached out again and unpacked the stars and made them dance like jewelled lightning across the dark face of the sky. All this she saw as she closed her eyes until she, too, was lulled and lost in a sleep of dreams.

THE KING OF THE BLUE LAGOON

Ann Turnbull

When Sally was at the seaside she found a stone on the beach. It was grey and oval and smoothed by the waves and it just filled the palm of her hand. Sally knew at once that it was a magic stone. She kept it in her pocket.

One day when Sally was skipping in the school playground the stone bounced out of her pocket and fell – plop! – into a puddle.

The puddle changed. It changed from a grey rainy-day puddle to a pool of deep, deep blue, with pink rocks in it, and glinting fish that flicked between them. Sally heard the boom and hiss of the surf. She put her hand into the water. It was warm and she felt a tickle of fish.

Her stone lay at the bottom. Sally took it out, and at once the blue sea, the surf, the pink rocks and glinting fish all vanished. And from Sally's hand came a voice that sighed,

"Far from the coral caves
Far from the sea
A witch's magic has enchanted me."

Sally put the stone back in her pocket. She looked around. No one else had noticed.

When she got home she took the stone into the garden. In the garden was a pond, with rocks around the edge and a plastic gnome fishing at the side.

Sally put the stone into the pond.

The water turned deep, deep blue, the rocks became a coral reef, the gnome turned into a mermaid who combed her hair and sang wild songs.

Sally took the stone out.

The blue sea, the coral reef and the mermaid all vanished and Sally heard a voice that sighed,

"Far from the coral caves

Far from the sea

A witch's magic has enchanted me."

That night, Sally put the stone into her bath.

The bath water turned deep, deep blue. The bath foam turned to sea foam. The soap became an angel fish. The flannel became a manta ray. An island with palm trees grew out of the soap dish. On Sally's plastic boat a pirate crew hoisted the Jolly Roger. Sally launched a Spanish galleon, laden with gold. There was a battle and cannon boomed across the water.

And all the time the stone lay at the bottom of the bath and Sally's mother hadn't noticed anything.

Sally took the stone out. At once the blue sea, the angel fish, the Spaniards and pirates all vanished and she heard a voice that sighed,

"Far from the coral caves

Far from the sea

A witch's magic has enchanted me."

After that, Sally always put the stone into her bath. But although the water changed and the boats changed and the soap and soap dish changed, the stone never changed. It lay on the bottom, cold and sad, and when Sally took it out, it always sighed,

"Far from the coral caves

Far from the sea

A witch's magic has enchanted me."

One day Sally went to the seaside again. She took the stone with her.

Sally waded into the sea, holding the stone in her

cupped hands. She squatted, and the sea washed over the stone and rocked it against her fingers.

The sea was a grey, cold sea. Sally thought it would change, but it didn't. Nothing changed. The sea was grey; the rocks were grey; the sky was grey.

But suddenly, in Sally's hands, the stone came alive. It twitched. It wiggled. It slithered and slipped. Sally looked down and saw that the stone had changed to a fish: a bright, bright fish with a rose-red body and turquoise stripes, golden eyes with black rims, fins that flicked silver and a rose-red shimmering tail. On its head was a crown.

"Oh!" said Sally. She was so surprised that she opened her fingers and the fish slipped through.

Before she could catch it, it flicked its tail and wiggled its body and swam away, bright as a jewel in the grey sea. Sally watched it grow smaller, and smaller, until at last it was no bigger than a sequin. Then it disappeared.

Sally felt something scraping and bumping against her foot. She bent down and picked up a shell. It was a big shell, pale pink and spiralled, that looked as if it had come from a blue sea far away.

Sally waded back to the shore, holding her shell. She knew at once that it was a magic shell. She showed it to her mother.

"You can hear the sea in a shell," said Sally's mother.

Sally held the shell to her ear. She heard the sea. She heard the boom and hiss of far-off surf. And above the sound of the surf she heard a glad voice, singing:

"Deep in the coral caves
Under the sea
King of the blue lagoon now I am free."